THE MACHINE
OF **DOOM**

Published by Ladybird Books Ltd 2012
A Penguin Company
Penguin Books Ltd, 80 Strand, London, WC2R 0RL, UK
Penguin Group (USA) Inc., 375 Hudson Street, New York 10014, USA
Penguin Books Australia Ltd, Camberwell Road, Camberwell, Victoria 3124,
Australia (A division of Pearson Australia Group Pty Ltd)
Canada, India, New Zealand, South Africa

Written by Cavan Scott
Illustrated by Dani Geremia – Beehive Illustration Agency
Sunbird is a trademark of Ladybird Books Ltd

www.ladybird.com

ISBN: 978-1-40939-118-0
001 – 10 9 8 7 6 5 4 3 2 1
Printed in Great Britain

THE MACHINE OF DOOM

by Onk Beakman

SUNBIRD
PENGUIN

CONTENTS

1 DANGER FROM THE SKIES..............7

2 CRASH!..............16

3 MABU MARKET..............23

4 THE SPELL PUNK..............39

5 THE MAP..............51

6 THE FOREST OF FEAR..............65

7 THE STUFF OF NIGHTMARES..............76

8 THE CHATTERING KEY..............90

9 THE TRAP..............99

10 THE PYRAMID OF JUST REWARDS..112

11 BEHOLD, THE MACHINE OF DOOM....124

12 A TRAP WITHIN A TRAP..............137

13 ESCAPE..............148

EPILOGUE..............158

CHAPTER ONE

DANGER FROM THE SKIES

Spyro the Dragon was worried. This would be his biggest challenge yet. As a Skylander, Spyro had faced all manner of terrors. He'd seen off armies of chaotic cyclopses, ghastly ghosts and wicked wizards, yet nothing compared to the horror that lay ahead. The mere thought of what was to come was enough to make his scales tremble.

Gill Grunt was about to sing.

Now this probably doesn't sound too bad.

Everyone loves a good tune after all, but Gill was a Gillman. In fact, Gill was the bravest Gillman Spyro had ever met. Together they had protected Skylands from evil and tyranny on countless occasions. And, after a tough day righting wrongs and generally being heroic, Gill liked nothing more than to relax with a sing-song.

The snag was, like all gillmen, Gill was a dreadful singer. An appalling singer. The kind of singer that made you want to pull off your own ears rather than listen to another note. Not that this stopped him. Even though he sounded

like a bullfrog gargling rancid jelly, Gill honestly believed he was one of the greatest singers in history and his friends were just too fond of the delusional Gillman to tell him the truth.

Except Eruptor that is. Eruptor was a hot-headed lava monster who never shied away from speaking his mind. When he had learnt that Gill was celebrating their latest victory over the forces of darkness with a special concert, Eruptor had insisted that he would rather do something more fun – like boiling his own head.

Eruptor had finally agreed to attend Gill's musical extravaganza on the condition that Gill promised never to stage such an event again.

"And you're sure he's only murdering one song?" Eruptor rumbled, his face like thunder. "No medleys? No encores?"

"It'll be fine," Spyro insisted, almost convincing himself. "Isn't that right, Boomer?"

Unfortunately, the troll sitting to Spyro's right couldn't hear him as he was too busy shoving sticks of dynamite into his own ears, just in case.

A hush fell across the audience as a tall, regal figure swept towards the stage. This was Eon, the Portal Master who had first recruited Spyro into the ranks of the Skylanders, the band of brave heroes who protected Skylands from attack.

Spyro had met the old wizard while playing in the Summer Forest back home. With a wave of his hand, all those years ago, Eon had opened a portal to another world.

"This is Skylands, the very centre of the universe," the Portal Master had explained proudly, revealing thousands of floating islands suspended in an azure blue sky. "Here, all things are possible

and adventure lies around every corner."

"It's beautiful," Spyro said in awe.

"Indeed it is," Eon had agreed. "But unfortunately it is also in constant danger from terrible dark forces."

"Why?" Spyro had asked, "What do they want with it?"

"Control," came the grave reply. "From here, you can travel anywhere in the cosmos. If Evil managed to gain a foothold in Skylands no world would be safe."

"You talk about evil as if it's alive."

"Maybe it is," Eon had said sadly. "It gets stronger as I grow older. I have protected Skylands for centuries, but now I need help. Your help."

Spyro had agreed to become a Skylander there and then. Eon had transported the young dragon to his mystical citadel where he had met Gill, Eruptor and the others. From that day on they had fought horrors that threatened to turn his scales white. He'd never looked back.

"Skylanders," Eon boomed out, his voice magically amplified around the grounds of his citadel. "Thank you for coming to Gill's latest concert . . ."

"Gill's final concert!" Eruptor reminded from the front.

"I'm sure we're all looking forward to seeing what musical treat he has in store for us, so please put your hands together for Gill Grunt!"

To the sound of rather cautious applause, Gill walked out on the stage, beaming from fin to fin. With a wave of Eon's enchanted staff, sweet music filled the air and a growing sense of doom descended over the audience. Gill opened his mouth and . . .

. . . someone at the back of the

crowd screamed.

"That's a first," Eruptor snorted. "Usually they wait until after Gill's started singing."

"It's not Gill's singing that's the problem," Spyro said, looking up. "It's that!"

Eruptor followed Spyro's gaze. There, high in the sky, was a hot air balloon. That, in itself, wasn't unusual. Unlike Eon, not everyone in Skylands could open magical portals to jump from island to island, so most travelled in airships, from the smallest balloon to the largest galleon.

The problem with this particular balloon was that it was coming in fast. Too fast.

"It's out of control!" Spyro warned as the Skylanders scattered. Only Boomer didn't move. Spyro's heart sank when he realised that the troll had dozed off exactly where the balloon would crash!

CHAPTER TWO

CRASH!

"**B**oomer!" Spyro yelled. "Get out of the way!"

But Boomer couldn't hear, thanks to the sticks of dynamite that were still jammed in his ears.

The balloon was almost upon them. Spyro lowered his head and charged towards his little green friend. If Boomer wasn't going to move, he'd have to do it. With only seconds to spare, the dragon butted Boomer out of harm's way. Behind them, the balloon ploughed into the ground, its heavy wooden basket smashing through the stage.

Out of breath, Spyro slid to a halt beside the distinctly dazed Boomer.

"What did you do that for?" the bewildered troll snapped.

"Just trying to save your life, that's all."

"Eh?" Boomer yelled. "What did you say?"

Spyro rolled his eyes. "Boomer, take the dynamite out of your ears!"

"You what?"

"I said," Spyro shouted louder, "take the dynamite out of your ears!"

"I can't hear you," Boomer yelled back, pointing at his crammed lugholes. "I've got dynamite in my ears!"

Spyro left the troll trying to remove the explosives from his ear canals and ran over to the wreckage. Planks of wood were scattered everywhere and the balloon itself was completely shredded.

Gill pulled a large, rotund figure from the remains of the basket.

"I should have known," bellowed Eruptor, recognising the survivor. "Flynn, is there any vehicle you can't fly into the ground?"

"Cool it, hot stuff. If the best pilot in this or

any other world wasn't at the helm, we would

have really been in

trouble." The newcomer

flashed a lopsided grin.

Flynn was a Mabu, the

race of creatures that largely

populated Skylands. His

usually immaculate flying

outfit was covered in dirt,

but amazingly, despite

a few cuts and grazes,

Flynn had escaped unscathed. Perhaps it wasn't

that surprising. When it came to crashing, Flynn

had plenty of experience, although he would

never admit it. "That was some landing. Boom!"

"Some landing?" Spyro looked at where the

basket had ploughed through the gardens of

the citadel. "Look at the damage."

"Don't worry," Eruptor grinned. "If Flynn

had been a minute later, Gill's vocal chords would have done a lot worse."

But the Gillman wasn't listening. Instead, he was still scrambling around in the wreckage.

"There's someone else in here," he called, his voice muffled by the twisted wood.

"There is?" Flynn asked, before remembering his passenger. "There is! Is the little fellow all right?"

"No, the little fellow certainly is not," came a shrill voice from within the basket. "Somebody get me out of here!"

"Hugo?" called Spyro, recognising the voice. Things were getting stranger by the minute. Hugo was Eon's librarian and general assistant. He was also completely terrified of flying. It wasn't so much being in the air that bothered the little Mabu. It was the thought of plummeting helplessly back to earth. He was

the last person you'd expect to hitch a ride with Flynn. What had he been thinking?

"That's the last time I step into your basket," Hugo spluttered as Gill finally pulled him free.

"There's gratitude for you," huffed Flynn, crossing his arms across his expansive stomach. "Next time you need to warn the Skylanders of impending doom, don't come running to me."

"Impending doom?" repeated Eon as he approached the basket, his brow creased with a frown. "What happened, Hugo?"

"Oh Master Eon, it was horrible." Hugo nervously pushed his glasses back up on to his nose. "I've always said this was going to happen.

They've been planning it for years and now they've struck."

"Who's struck?" asked Spyro, fearing the worst. "Is it the ice ogres? Or the basilisks?" He paused for a minute as a terrible thought occurred to him. "Please don't say it's Kaos."

A groan went around the assembled Skylanders. Kaos was their arch-enemy, an evil Portal Master who was always trying to conquer Skylands.

"No, it's even worse than that, Spyro. Skylands is under attack . . ."

No one dared to even breathe as Hugo paused for dramatic effect.

"... from sheep!"

CHAPTER THREE

MABU MARKET

"**Y**ou're joking?" Spyro couldn't help but laugh. "All of this is because of a few sheep?"

"Oh you can mock, young Skylander," scolded Hugo, wagging his finger at the dragon. "But I always told you this day would come."

Even Eon allowed himself a wry smile. "Hugo, how many times do we need to go through this?" the Portal Master asked. "You have nothing to fear from sheep. They're harmless."

Hugo couldn't believe his ears. "That's what they want you to think. 'Look at those gentle little lambs. Aren't they cute? Aren't they cuddly?' But they're not. They're merciless mounds of mutton and now they can fly, there'll be no stopping them."

Eruptor shook his head in disbelief. "Wait a minute. Now they can fly? I think somebody hit their head when they fell out of the sky."

"The little fellow may not appreciate a good pilot when he sees one, but he's not wrong," chipped in Flynn. "I wouldn't have believed it if I hadn't seen it with my own peepers."

"You actually saw sheep fly?" asked Gill, "But that's . . ."

". . . impossible, I know. If you ask me the only things that should fly are birds, dragons and unbelievably handsome pilots!"

"This is most irregular," said Eon, stroking his beard. "Hugo, you had better start at the beginning."

"Well, the citadel's larders were running low, so I popped over to Mabu Market," began Hugo. "I was happily browsing the stalls, when something swooped over my head. I stumbled and my glasses fell on the floor. There I was trying to find them when this blundering ignoramus barged into me."

"Hey, less of the 'blundering'," Flynn retorted. "I was just shocked, that's all."

"You were screaming like a little girl, that's what you were doing," Hugo insisted. "'They're after me Hugo, they're after me.' Sound familiar?"

"Fair's fair," Flynn sniffed, self-consciously straightening his scarf. "It's not every day you get dive-bombed by levitating livestock!"

"You mean the sheep?" asked Spyro.

"Yes, I mean the sheep," confirmed Hugo. "I found my glasses, only to see the dreadful things soaring through the air like woolly vultures, grabbing all and sundry with razor-sharp talons."

"Sheep with talons?" repeated Gill, gulping hard.

"Well, hooves," admitted Hugo, "but it's much the same thing."

"Come, Skylanders." Eon strode towards the citadel doors. "We must see this for ourselves." Spyro and the others followed the Portal Master into the main hall where a huge portal of power sat on a raised platform. Eon ascended the stairs and swept his staff across the ancient device.

"Portal," he commanded, "show me Mabu Market."

A ghostly image appeared on the surface of the plinth. It was faint at first, but soon shimmered into focus.

"Mabu Market," Spyro whispered, unable to believe what he was seeing, "but it's completely wrecked."

"Are you sure that Flynn didn't just crash into it?" asked Eruptor, as he shoved his way through.

"I heard that," called out Flynn from the back.

"Now will you believe me?" asked Hugo. "It's those dratted sheep."

Spyro frowned. "I don't know, Hugo. I can't see . . ."

A blurred, white shape flashed across the image.

"There's one," Hugo yelled out excitedly. "And another. Did you see?"

Suddenly the skies above the marketplace

were filled with indistinguishable white blobs.

"Maybe Hugo's right . . ." admitted Gill, rubbing his fins nervously.

"There's only one way to be sure," Eon decided. "Spyro, Gill and Eruptor, you must go to Mabu Market and discover what is really happening."

"What about me?" chipped in Boomer, "I haven't blown anything up all day."

Eon shook his head. "Not this time Boomer. Flynn will need your help repairing his balloon."

With a wave of his staff, Eon primed the portal. It hummed with energy, the strange symbols carved into its rough stone sides glowing brightly before a column of blinding light erupted up to the high, vaulted ceiling.

"You know the drill," yelled Gill, strapping on his trusty water cannon and jumping headfirst into the portal. "Last one there's a tadpole!"

Gill Grunt had never really understood Hugo's aversion to sheep. If it had been trolls then he would totally get it. The only troll Gill trusted was Boomer who, save for his love of explosives, had turned his back on the troll lifestyle. On the whole, trolls were nasty pieces of work. Their hobbies included war, bullying and hiding bombs in each other's pants. These were the kind of creatures whose idea of relaxing was sitting down with a map to work out which civilization to oppress next.

Unfortunately, trolls were also partial to barbecued fish. There had been plenty of times, even in the midst of battle, when Gill had spotted trolls giving him funny looks and licking their horrible, wet lips. He knew the green brutes were picturing him slowly basting over a roaring fire.

But sheep? As far as he knew sheep had never harmed anyone, save for the time they munched their way through Hugo's cabbage patch.

That was until today. The scene that greeted the Skylanders was one of total chaos. Stalls were upended and spoiled fruit and vegetables were being trampled into the ground by panicked Mabu.

But there were no sheep to be seen.

"Watch out!"

Gill turned to find himself staring into the startled eyes of a large, fat ewe. He tried to get out of the way, but couldn't move quickly enough and ended up with a mouthful of coarse, bitter-tasting wool. He was still choking on it when the sheep swept around and shot back to the debris-strewn market square.

"Sorry, Gill." Spyro whacked the spluttering Gillman on the back. "I tried to warn you."

"This is just weird," said Eruptor as they watched a flock of flying sheep streak over the collapsed stalls in a perfect arrow formation. "How are they doing it?"

"I'm not sure," admitted Spyro. "It's not as if they've sprouted wings or anything."

"So what are we going to do?" asked Gill, finally clearing his throat.

"Why don't you try blasting them with your water cannon," suggested Spyro, taking to the air himself as three sheep soared a little too close for comfort. "See if you can slow them down a bit."

"Great idea," yelled Gill, his eyes sparkling as he aimed the nozzle of his water cannon in the direction of an incoming flock. "It's time for

a wash down."

A column of water gushed from Gill's cannon, hitting one of the approaching sheep

right between the eyes. The force of the water knocked the animal sideways and it dropped like a very soggy stone.

"Good shot," praised Eruptor as they ran to where the sheep lay on its back, legs wiggling helplessly in the air. Its drenched wool had absorbed most of the water and had swollen to twice its normal size.

Spyro gently butted the animal back on its feet. It stood for a second until its trembling knees gave out under the weight of its waterlogged wool and it collapsed once again with a splat. Gill prodded the creature with the barrel of his cannon.

"This is one low-flying lamb chop that is well and truly grounded," he reported proudly.

"What are you waiting for?" asked Eruptor, "Soak 'em all."

Gill didn't get a chance to answer. He was

too busy landing on his behind as the sopping sheep suddenly leapt from the ground, smacked Gill in the face for the second time that day and took off back into the air, with a bleat that sounded as surprised as they were.

"I thought you said that thing couldn't fly any more?" barked Eruptor, as he dodged the dripping dive-bomber.

"Well, excuse me for not being an expert in soaring sheep." Gill spat out a lump of matted wool. "I don't see you coming up with any clever ideas."

"Guys!" Spyro jumped in between his two squabbling friends. "We haven't got time for this."

It was at that point that the banana hit Spyro on the nose.

The banana was followed by an apple, then a peach and then an orange. Before they knew

it, the Skylanders were being pelted from all angles. Fruit and veg were flying everywhere.

"First sheep and then this?" yelled Eruptor who was quickly being smothered in fruit pulp. "Who's throwing this stuff anyway?"

Spyro tried to look, ducking sharply to avoid an incoming pumpkin. "There's no-one there. It's just picking itself off the ground and chucking itself at us."

"I've heard of tossed salad," Gill cried out, scraping tomato seeds from his eyes, "but this is ridiculous. Can today get any worse?"

"Funny you should say that," Eruptor was staring at Gill's trousers. "Do you know you've got dynamite shoved in your belt?"

CHAPTER FOUR

THE SPELL PUNK

Gill's eyes stretched even wider than usual. Sure enough, tucked into his waistband was a stick of dynamite, its fuse lit and sparking away merrily. With a cry of alarm, the Gillman snatched the explosive out of his belt.

"What are you waiting for?" bellowed Eruptor. "Get rid of it!"

Gill didn't need to be told twice. He pitched his arm back and threw the dynamite as far away as possible. It bounced off a perplexed-looking ram and exploded in mid-air, sending the slightly singed farm animal shooting off at a tangent.

More explosions boomed all around as the remaining stalls were suddenly consumed by balls of flame. Spyro threw up his front claws to protect his face from flying shrapnel and charred cucumbers.

"I don't get it," he said, as another stall was reduced to splinters by a blast. "First the sheep, then the fruit and now this. Nothing about this makes sense."

"This isn't doing my indigestion any good at all," Eruptor complained before burping out molten lava on to the ground in front of them.

"Pardon."

Spyro only just jumped out of the way before his toes could be fried, but someone – or something – wasn't so lucky. To the Skylanders' amazement, steaming footprints appeared in the pool of magma. There was a shrill shriek and the footprints continued across the lava and into the grass before vanishing not a metre from where the Skylanders were standing.

"Did you see that?" exclaimed Gill.

Spyro nodded. "But what was it?"

"I've got an idea. Quick, scoop as much of this fruit into my pack as you can."

Spyro and Eruptor looked at each other, shrugged and did what Gill asked, scraping the fruit mush from the ground and slopping it into the pack that fed the Gillman's water cannon.

As soon as they'd finished, Gill started jiggling about on the spot. Water sloshed everywhere

as Eruptor looked on in bewilderment. "This isn't the time for a dance-off, fish fingers."

"Watch and learn, rock face," said Gill, spinning on his heels and raising his cannon towards a nearby trio of hovering sheep. "Watch and learn."

As Gill's finger tightened around the trigger, a gloopy stream of multicoloured sludge squirted from the cannon. The sheep bleated in alarm, but relaxed as it shot beneath their flailing legs.

"You missed!" Eruptor said in disbelief. "You never miss. That sheep must have hit you harder than we thought."

"He wasn't aiming for the sheep," called Spyro over the roar of the cannon. "Look."

"The sheep weren't flying," Gill shouted triumphantly as the sludge slammed into something just beneath the startled ewes. "They were just being carried by invisible trolls."

Eruptor's mouth dropped open. Sure enough, three stocky figures had appeared out of thin air, dripping with Gill's slimy fruit cocktail. The mucky mixture had coated their see-through

bodies, making them visible again.

The three sticky silhouettes looked at each other, realised they could be seen and fled, discarding their sheep as they ran.

Gill span in a circle, dousing the entire marketplace in pulp. More concealed trolls were revealed wherever the goo splashed.

"Since when have they been able to make themselves invisible?" Spyro wondered, as the newly visible trolls beat a hasty retreat, slipping on pulverized fruit as they scrabbled to get away. "How are they doing it?"

"Who cares?" replied Eruptor with a grin. "If we can see them we can fight back! Time for them to feel the burn!"

The lava monster raised his glowing fists and let loose a barrage of lava blobs. At least two of the scampering trolls yelped, shot into the air and clutched their seared behinds.

Spyro was about to join the fight when he spotted something out of the corner of his eye. A figure broke cover from a pile of discarded pallets and darted across the marketplace. It was small, hovered a foot or so off the ground and wore a large, pointed hat. Spyro growled. It could only be one thing – a spell punk.

Spell punks were loathsome wizards who only used their magic to cause mischief. Worst of all, most of them worked for Kaos. If a spell punk had turned the trolls invisible, then the treacherous Portal Master was probably behind the attack on the market. But what could Kaos possibly want with a few fruit and vegetable stalls?

Whatever Kaos was plotting, the spell punk would have the answers. Leaving Gill and Eruptor to deal with the trolls, Spyro flew after the mischievous mage and was soon snapping

at its flapping robes. Panicking, the wizard scooped up a handful of grapes from a stall and flung them back into Spyro's eyes. The dragon stumbled for a second, swatting the fruit away, but it was just long enough for the spell punk to change direction and nip into the old clock tower that stood in the middle of Mabu Market. It glanced nervously back and slammed the door shut.

Spyro smiled. The only way the spell punk could go was up. The dragon shot up the side of the clock tower, dived through a window to the belfry and waited for the spell punk at the top of the spiral staircase.

The wizard turned to run back down the stairs but was too late. Spyro pounced and pinned

the struggling punk to the cold, stone floor.

"I told the trolls this would happen," the spell punk screamed in frustration. "We just needed to test the invisibility spell, but they would insist on playing their stupid games, drawing attention to themselves."

"But why does Kaos need an invisibility spell in the first place? What is he planning?"

"Well, how else do you expect him to get his hands on the Chattering Key?" the spell punk asked before his eyes went wide. "Oops. I wasn't supposed to mention that!"

"The Chattering Key?" Spyro snapped back.

"What's the Chattering Key?"

But the spell punk wasn't listening. He was staring mournfully over Spyro's shoulder, where a dark, swirling storm cloud had appeared from nowhere. Lightning flashed across the sky as a giant, glowering face materialised in the centre of the maelstrom. Spyro's eyes narrowed – it was the face of Kaos!

"IDIOT!" Kaos boomed, his voice so loud that it rattled the bricks of the clock tower. "I knew you couldn't be trusted."

"M-master, I'm sorry," the spell punk stammered. "I didn't think . . ."

"You never do, that's the problem. I am surrounded by nincompoops!" Kaos bawled. "You just wait till I get you home! You are DOOOOOMED!"

With a strangled sob, the spell punk disintegrated into a puff of dark, foul-smelling

smoke. Spyro raced to the window and watched as all the fruit-splattered trolls also vanished, transported back to Kaos's lair.

Spyro hurled himself out of the window and was immediately buffeted by gale force winds. He flapped his wings furiously to avoid being dashed against the clock tower.

From the eye of the storm, Kaos bellowed with laughter.

"And to think I was worried that Eon's sorry band of Skylanders would ruin my plans. Ha! You can hardly even fly."

Spyro stared defiantly into the eyes of his enemy. He wasn't beaten yet.

"What is the Chattering Key?" he yelled, his voice cracking as he struggled to be heard over the ever-increasing tempest, "and why do you want it so badly?"

Kaos just grinned.

"That's for me to know, little dragonfly," the evil Portal Master sneered, "and for you to find out. Farewell Skyblunderers!"

And with that Kaos' face shimmered away to nothing and the dark clouds parted to reveal shards of brilliant sunlight. Exhausted, Spyro half-tumbled down to where his friends were waiting. They needed to get back to Eon.

CHAPTER FIVE

THE MAP

The library beneath Eon's citadel was big. Really big. In fact, it was so big that it was said you didn't just need a map to navigate its labyrinthine corridors and endless sections – you needed an entire atlas. Hugo claimed that he even tried to cross the library on foot once. Three years into his trek he'd only reached the 'C' section, before giving up and trudging back to the front desk.

While Spyro wasn't sure he believed Hugo's tall tale, Eon had installed a network of portals so that the little historian could jump from one section to another without wearing out a lifetime's supply of shoe leather.

As soon as Spyro had mentioned the Chattering Key on his return to the citadel, Hugo had leapt into action. Granted, he'd instantly tripped on his own shoelace and landed flat on his face. However, as soon as he'd dusted himself down, he had scrambled onto the nearest portal and zipped off to the 'Arcane Artefacts and Otherworldly Objects' section (which apparently was just next to 'The History of Plumbing' and 'Break Dancing').

"Kaos, eh?" Flynn muttered

beneath his breath as they waited for Hugo to return. Thanks to Boomer's help, the dashing-if-bungling pilot had finished repairs on his ship, but had insisted on staying behind as soon as he'd heard that Kaos was involved. Like all in Skylands, Flynn hated the villainous Portal Master. "That guy really pumps my propellers. I'd like to fly my balloon right into that stupid, big head of his. Boom!"

"It's not even his real face," complained Eruptor, who was still picking scorched strawberries from his arms. "He's fooling no-one. We know he's just a useless little twerp behind all those special effects."

"Kaos may not be the tallest fellow, but it would be unwise to dismiss him as useless."

Eon strode into the library, his pristine silver robes sweeping across the highly polished floor.

"Aw, come on boss," said Boomer. "You could take that pipsqueak any day of the week. He's seriously small fry. Plus, that troll he hangs with, Glumshanks? I heard that he flunked everything back in the Troll academy, from rudimentary detonation to advanced annihilation. He couldn't even work out which end of the dynamite to light."

Eon lowered himself into an elegant chair and rubbed the bridge of his long nose. Spyro frowned. The Portal Master was looking so tired, so weary. The others were right to a degree. Kaos was, at a basic level, a bit of a joke. But he was an increasingly powerful joke. Spyro had to admit that the cowled head that had appeared in the clouds above the market was terrifying. It had looked like Kaos, but all the features had been heightened. They were sharper, more imposing and brimming with

malevolence. Kaos was getting stronger and over the last few years had certainly been living up to his name.

Hugo had once told Spyro that Kaos had been born into a royal family, but while his brothers were blessed with long, flowing locks, good looks and devastating charm, Kaos was bald, ugly and devastatingly smelly. When his father dismissed him as an embarrassing runt, Kaos renounced his family and fled into the wilderness, alone and friendless (unless you count his faithful butler, Glumshanks, that is). Desperate for companionship of the non-troll variety, he set to work on trying to build friends of his own out of wood. Remarkably, he actually had some success, and thus the mannequin people known as the Wilikin were born. Unfortunately, Kaos being Kaos, even his own creations could not bear to be around him.

Despite being equipped with no sense of smell, the Wilikin were nonetheless able to detect their creator's distinctive pong, and ran off to become servants for the royal family. It wasn't all bad news for Kaos, however. Having created the Wilikin, he realized he had something of a knack for magic, and he threw himself into learning more about this unexpected power. When his research brought him to the subject of Portal Masters, he immediately knew he must be one of them. The only problem was, he didn't have a portal. So, with Glumshanks at his side, he began to scour the universe for one.

It was only a matter of time before they found their way to Skylands and learnt of the Core of Light, the mysterious machine that filled Skylands with light and kept Darkness at bay. Hungry for power, Kaos had tried to destroy the Core there and then, but had been defeated by

Eon and the Skylanders. Unfortunately, the evil Portal Master had never given up on the dream of grinding Skylands beneath his stinking boot.

Spyro shuddered at the thought. If Skylands fell, the universe would follow.

"Are you alright, Master?" Spyro asked, padding up to the Portal Master. "You look tired."

A weary smile stretched across Eon's face, banishing a little of the tension. "I am tired, Spyro, but it's nothing a good night's sleep wouldn't solve. Don't worry yourself. All is well."

"I'm not so sure about that!" Hugo appeared in a flare of light from the middle of the Portal. The squat scholar was clutching a cumbersome book that was almost as big as he was. He squeaked with alarm when it threatened to topple over and squash him against the Portal's surface.

"Just a little light reading, eh Hugo," Gill quipped as he rushed to assist the historian.

"If only, Gill," replied Hugo. "There is nothing trivial about the objects catalogued in this book."

Spyro flapped around to look over Hugo's shoulder. "Professor P. Grungally's Rise and Fall of the Ancient Arkeyans, volume 817," he read. "How many volumes are there?"

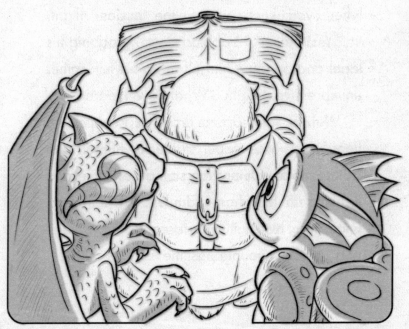

"At last count, somewhere in the region of 2,000."

"And you've read every one?"

"Twice, as it happens. They get a bit stale around volume 1,462, but pick up by the end."

"I'm sure all of this is fascinating," grumbled Eruptor, "but have you learnt anything about this Chattering Key thing?" Eruptor was never one for reading. It's hard to flick through a paperback when you keep setting the pages alight.

"Yes, indeed," babbled Hugo, grabbing his lapel and bringing himself up to his full, rather unimpressive, height. "What have I learnt?"

With a sigh, Spyro dropped back to the floor. Hugo was about to launch himself into lecture mode. Other than stamp collecting and quaking in fear from harmless lawn-grazers, imparting his not-inconsiderable knowledge was Hugo's favourite pastime.

"Well," he began, hardly drawing breath, "as you know, Skylands was once ruled by the terrible Arkeyans..."

"Yes, yes, yes," interrupted Eruptor. "We know. Evil sorcerer kings, lived in dark and dusty underground cities, built thousands of enchanted weapons of mass destruction and were sealed in a vault of eternal sleep after a battle to end all battles, yadda, yadda, yadda."

Hugo fixed the lava monster with an icy stare. "I'm sorry if I'm boring you, but it appears the Arkeyans also created the Chattering Key that Kaos seems so keen to get his grubby little mitts on."

"A key to what?" asked Spyro.

"A very good question, Skylander."

"Any chance of a good answer?" Eruptor glared back at the historian.

Hugo sniffed and turned to Spyro, ignoring the lava monster. "I'm afraid no-one knows. All Professor Grungally says is that it's a 'mysterious, ancient Arkeyan artefact rumoured to open an even more mysterious, ancient Arkeyan tomb that possibly contains an infinitely more mysterious, ancient Arkeyan weapon."

"Just the kind of thing the Kaos creep is always searching for," mused Flynn.

"Exactly."

"And what's the betting that Professor Smartypants fails to mention where this mysterious, ancient artefact is hidden?" complained Eruptor to a sniggering Boomer. The troll always enjoyed a little bit of Hugo-baiting.

"You're correct," admitted Hugo, a slight smile playing across his thin lips. "Unfortunately, the

Professor doesn't know the location of the key . . ."

"Told you!"

"But I do!"

With a flourish, Hugo pulled an old scroll from his satchel and brandished it like a trophy.

"Is that a map?" asked Spyro excitedly.

Maps meant adventure. Sure, they also usually meant life-threatening danger and hideous monsters, but that came with the territory.

"No, it's my shopping list," snapped Hugo. "Of course it's a map."

"So, where's the key?" inquired Gill, licking his lips at the prospect of a new mission.

Hugo unrolled the map and laid it across the open book.

The surface of the brittle parchment was shaded green, indicating areas of dense vegetation, except for a central clearing marked by a big, red cross. A grin spread across Spyro's face. A treasure hunt – his favourite kind of adventure.

"Don't get too excited, Spyro." Eon had risen from his chair and walked to gaze down at the map. "If I'm correct, that is one of the most perilous islands in all of Skylands."

Hugo nodded gravely. "You're right Master. The Chattering Key lies at the heart of the Forest of Fear."

CHAPTER SIX

THE FOREST OF FEAR

"**B**race yourself!"

Gill swallowed hard.

"Is it just me . . ." the Gillman said, a slight warble in his voice betraying his nervousness. "Or does that ground look like it's coming in really fast?"

"Oh, I don't know," replied Spyro, with little in the way of confidence. "I'm sure Flynn knows what he's doing."

"I have absolutely no idea what I'm doing,"

shouted Flynn from the controls of the airship, "but it sure is fun."

"We're going to crash!" shouted Boomer excitedly, almost beside himself with glee.

"And that's a good thing, why?" whined Eruptor.

"Because it'll make a huge boom!" Boomer cheered, jumping up and down and making the oversized basket shake even more. Eruptor just moaned. The fiery Skylander had been feeling airsick since leaving Eon's citadel, a fact that continued to worry Spyro. Wicker baskets and monsters that vomit up burning pools of molten lava don't go well together.

"I still don't understand why we couldn't just take a portal to the Forest of Fear?" Eruptor groaned, looking decidedly green.

"Because the Forest is surrounded by thick mist-storms," Spyro explained for the

one-hundredth time. "Master Eon can only create a portal if he can see where we're heading. The fog's just too dense."

"So's our pilot," shot back Eruptor as the balloon lurched violently.

"If I wasn't so busy trying to keep us in the sky, I would take that personally," Flynn yelled, randomly pulling this lever and yanking that, none of which seemed to make the slightest difference to their descent.

"Grab hold of something," warned Gill, holding on to the side of the basket and screwing his eyes shut. "Here comes the ground in all its bone-breaking glory!"

Eruptor screamed. Gill screamed. Even Flynn screamed. Boomer giggled, but he'd always been a little odd. Spyro, meanwhile, couldn't take his eyes away from the rocks that were spinning towards them. Of course, he could

have just flown out of the basket, but then he would have been in danger of getting tangled in the coarse ropes that held the basket beneath the gigantic balloon. It couldn't end like this, he thought, as the airship spiralled down. All the adventure, all the magic and they'd meet their end in a balloon crash. It didn't seem fair.

At the last minute, Spyro turned away and closed his eyes, waiting for the inevitable impact.

It never came.

Cautiously, Spyro opened one eye. They were all still in the basket. He opened the other. They were safe. The basket wasn't falling any more. It was hovering just inches from the ground and, with the gentlest of bumps, touched down.

"Skylanders, this is your captain speaking. You may unbuckle your safety straps as we have reached our destination."

"Safety straps," Eruptor spluttered. "You

never told us there were safety straps."

"Nah," said Flynn, who was contentedly powering down the furnace. "Never use 'em."

"But we didn't crash!" blurted out Boomer, actually sounding disappointed.

"Of course we didn't. I don't always crash," insisted Flynn, ignoring the look that every one of the Skylander's flashed him. "Besides, I'd never noticed this before."

"Noticed what?" asked Gill, finally letting go of the basket.

"This little control here." He moved in closer to closer to peer at the label. "'Flip this lever to land without crashing'". Who knew?"

Spyro shook his head and leapt out of the basket. "Come on guys. We've got work to do."

"Personally, I'll just be happy if I never set foot in that basket again," said Eruptor as he clambered out.

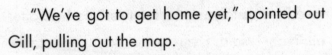

"We've got to get home yet," pointed out Gill, pulling out the map.

"Maybe I'll just stay here."

"I wouldn't want to," admitted Boomer, as he gazed into the thick overgrowth that stood before them. Gnarled trees twisted into the sky, craggy bark covered by open sores that oozed sap the colour of mouldy cheese. High above, a canopy of dry, dead leaves blocked what little sunlight remained, casting a gloomy shadow across the forest floor. All around them strange cries filled the air. Spyro couldn't shake the feeling that he was being watched from every jagged branch.

"OK, Gill," Spyro said, trying to sound more confident than he felt. "Where do we find this key?"

"Straight on," replied Gill, consulting the map. "Into the forest."

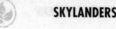
" Perhaps Flynn's balloon isn't so bad after all."

The Skylanders were keeping close together as they pushed their way through the undergrowth. The path ahead, if that's what you could call the carpet of vicious-looking brambles and painful nettles, was lit by Eruptor's flame, but even the lava monster's glare seemed dull and weak. It was if the forest was absorbing every last scrap of light.

"Are you sure we're still going in the right direction?" Spyro asked, jumping slightly as something long, slimy and with too many legs crawled over his foot.

"I think so." Gill peered at the old parchment. "Not that I can really see anything in this gloom. We just need to keep pushing forward."

"I could always clear the way ahead," offered Boomer. "All it would take is a few bombs. Twenty-three at the most."

"No." Spyro cut off the troll before he could start lighting fuses. "If Kaos is after the key, we don't want him to know we're here."

Wrinkling his nose, Gill lowered the map.

"What's that terrible smell?"

"Sorry," said Eruptor. "My stomach's still not right since that journey."

"No, that's not it," continued Gill. "It's musty, like damp earth. The closer we get to the clearing, the more moisture is in the air. I can feel it in my gills."

"Wow! Look at these," cried out Boomer, stopping to study the forest floor.

"It's quite pretty whatever it is," said Gill, turning back to join his molten comrade. "Looks like some kind of fungi."

"They're all over the place," pointed out Eruptor. The lava monster was right. Brightly coloured fungus was popping up all over the

forest floor. Each was a different colour – vibrant reds, greens and yellows – and all were inflating as if filling with gas.

"Hey, I've just noticed something," said Gill, looking back at the map. "If I'm right we're standing in an area called 'The Fungus Rings of Despair'. Is it just me or does that not sound good to you?"

Spyro didn't have a chance to answer. Without warning the scarlet fungus he was examining burst, sending a plume of mist into his face. The world went dark.

CHAPTER **SEVEN**

THE STUFF OF NIGHTMARES

Gill's stomach rumbled as he started to wake up. "Mmmmm," he thought to himself, as he struggled to open his eyes. "Something smells good. I wonder what's for breakfast?"

He tried to stretch but found he couldn't move his arms. He must have been tucked into bed tightly last night. Odd. There was something else. His bedroom was roasting. Perhaps he'd gone to sleep with the heating on. It didn't matter. He'd turn it off again when he'd polished off

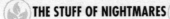
that delicious-smelling breakfast. What was that smell? Bacon? No. Kippers. Yes, that was it...

Kippers? Gill's eyes sprung open and he remembered. He wasn't in bed and the heating wasn't on. Worst of all, it wasn't kippers sizzling away for breakfast. It was him!

The troll giggled in anticipation as he turned the spit over the open campfire. Gill struggled against his bonds, but the ropes were too tight. The heat was unbearable.

A second troll appeared and started to shake something over Gill. The Gillman choked as the seasoning went in his eyes and mouth. Salt and pepper. This could only mean one thing . . .

Gill Grunt was being barbecued alive!

The Skylander threw back his head and screamed for help.

◆

Eruptor shivered. It was absolutely freezing. His teeth chattering, he forced his eyes open. The forest floor was covered in a blanket of crisp, white snow, with more falling all the time.

Eruptor looked all around him. Where were the others? Then he spotted the three lumps in the snow. They'd been buried alive! With a grunt, he tried to walk towards the first, smaller heap. That had to be Boomer. If he could get to the troll, he could dig him out and then rescue the others. But he couldn't move. The snow was up to his waist and his short, stubby legs weren't suited to traipsing through snowdrifts.

"Don't panic," the Skylander told himself. "You can just melt your way through." All he needed to do was cough up a red-hot magma ball. That would clear the snow. Eruptor hacked, but nothing happened. That wasn't right. He tried again, but still nothing.

"Must be getting a cold," Eruptor reasoned. "I'll try a lava blast from my hands. That'll do it." Eruptor clapped his fists together, expecting lava to gush forward, but nothing came. He tried again, and again, his heart racing despite the icy chill that cut through to his bones. In disbelief he looked at his shaking hands and his face fell even further. No, this couldn't be happening. It wasn't possible. As he watched, their glow was visibly fading, his skin hardening, cracking and cooling. He tried to lift his hands but found he could hardly move. His arms felt like solid rock and he was so, so cold.

A single tear escaped from Eruptor's eye and froze on his cheek. His worst fear had come true. His internal flame had gone out. The Skylander threw back his head and cried for help.

Boomer heard music. Pretty music. Girlie music. With a slight moan, he opened his eyes. What had happened? Had he been standing too near one of his own explosions? The troll shook his head to clear his vision and the world lurched back into view.

No, not this.

Boomer was sitting crossed-legged on a picnic blanket. Beside him, a basket was brimming with sandwiches, macaroons and fairy cakes.

All around him sat overstuffed teddy bears and dolls with blue eyes, rosebud mouths and cascading blond ringlets. As nursery rhymes played in the background, his hostess skipped up, a teapot clutched in one podgy little hand.

"Would you like more tea, Mr Troll?" the little angel asked as she twirled frizzy, ginger hair around a finger. To his horror, Boomer felt himself nodding and watched in terror as the girl poured liquid into the tiny china cup that lay at his feet.

Boomer tried to stop himself, but couldn't. He watched his own hand reach out and pick up the bright pink cup. Then, worst of all, his little finger sprung out as he daintily brought the cup to his lips.

He was trapped in a doll's tea party – the greatest nightmare of any troll brought to life.

Screaming with the effort, Boomer managed

to throw the teacup away from his lips and watched as it smashed into tiny pieces on a tree trunk. There was no way he was being kept here amongst all this . . . cuteness.

"Mr Troll," the little girl exclaimed, her pug nose creasing into a frown. "That was very naughty. Now I'm going to have to tidy up." With that, she clapped her hand and the tiny shards of china leapt back into the air where they re-formed into the cup. Seconds later it was back on the saucer in front of Boomer.

"I expect you'll want a top up," the girl asked, leaning forward with the teapot.

"No, I do not!" Boomer reached to where he kept his emergency explosives. "Let's see if you can tidy up from this, missy!"

With a cry of triumph, he whipped out a hand that should have been brandishing a fizzing stick of dynamite. The cry turned into a whimper. He wasn't clutching a primed explosive in his hand. Oh no. He was holding a beautiful, yellow carnation.

The little girl clapped delightedly. "Oh yes, Mr Troll, what a wonderful idea. Let's practise flower arranging."

The Skylander threw back his head and yelled for help.

Spyro could hear his friends screaming but couldn't help. He couldn't even move. It was if he'd been frozen, only able to move his eyes.

In front of him, Master Eon knelt on the forest floor, his long, slender fingers desperately clutching at the iron collar he wore around his neck. Spyro could see the rusty metal cutting into Eon's throat and hear his mentor's strangled cries, but could do nothing to help.

The chain connected to the iron collar was

yanked back and Eon tumbled on to his back to lay motionless in the brambles. Spyro's frustrated gaze followed the chain link by link until it reached the hand of the person who had done this.

Kaos.

This was Kaos as he really was – short, ugly and cruel. The strange little man gave another tug of the chain and Spyro heard Eon choke, a sound that only seemed to amuse the vile runt of a villain who placed a foot on the fallen Portal Master's chest.

"It's all mine," Kaos cackled, "Skylands. The Universe. Mine to do with as I will. The universe is doomed, I tell you, DOOOOOOMED!"

Spyro tried to shout out, but his jaw wouldn't move.

"Oh, is the little dragonfly trying to say something?" Kaos jeered. "Has he lost his voice? What a pity."

That was it. Spyro wasn't going to sit here and be insulted by Kaos, not while Eon lay helpless on the floor. Summoning all his energy, Spyro closed his eyes and forced his mouth to move.

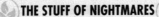

"Get . . . away . . . from . . . Eon," he hissed through gritted fangs.

"What? This pathetic old man?" Kaos cocked a quizzical eyebrow, while continuing to grind his foot into the Portal Master's chest. "And what exactly are you going to do if I don't? Stare me to death? You are NOTHING, little dragon and I am EVERYTHING!"

Spyro could feel his anger burning deep in his belly. He let it grow, feeding it with thoughts of what he would do if he got to Kaos, until it burst out of his mouth in a huge ball of fire. The pain in his jaw was immense, but he didn't care. He needed to save Eon.

Kaos's eyes stretched in panic as the flames roared towards him. The little wizard threw his hands in front of his face and then vanished as the fireball passed through him. Spyro blinked and realized Eon was gone too. Now all he could see was the brightly coloured fungus on the forest floor, each furiously pumping spores into the air.

The fungus. That was it. This nightmare had started when Spyro had been blasted in the face. What had Gill said they were called: 'The Fungus Rings of Despair'? The spores must have affected his brain and made him believe his worst nightmares had come true. Ever since he'd met Eon he'd been afraid that one day the old man would fall to Kaos.

But that's all it was, an irrational fear. Spyro realised that he could move again and turned to see all three of his friends trapped in their own nightmares. Eruptor was curled up in a shivering ball, Gill was rolling over and over on the ground and Boomer was yelling "No, not the daisies! Anything but the daisies!"

Springing forward, Spyro cut a path through

the fungi with his flaming breath, reducing the hallucinogenic plants to a crisp. Eruptor, Gill and Boomer blinked and looked around.

"What happened?" Gill asked.

"I'll explain later," Spyro called back, shooting ahead into the trees. "We need to get out of these rings before the fungi grow back."

His friends didn't need telling twice. Still shaken by their experiences they chased after Spyro, although Boomer did pause just to check he had T.N.T. in his pockets and not Hydrangeas.

CHAPTER EIGHT

THE CHATTERING KEY

"According to the map," said Gill, pushing through the undergrowth without looking where he was going, "the Chattering Key is just through this clearing."

"Gill, get down." Without warning, Boomer reached up and slammed the Gillman down with one of his heavy, green hands."

"Ow!" Gill cried out. "What did you do that for?"

"I can smell trolls," Boomer hissed.

"Boomer," Eruptor barged past, eager to get this adventure over and done with. "How many times have we got to tell you this? The reason you can smell trolls is because you are a troll."

"No," said Spyro, frozen to the spot. "He's right. Look."

The four friends peered through the trees. Two squat trolls were stalking towards the statue of a huge wyvern that sat on top of an imposing black pyramid in the middle of the clearing.

"Check out what's around that thing's neck," whispered Gill. "That has to be the key."

Sure enough, hanging from a chain around the stone wyvern's neck, was a huge key, complete with a metal face moulded into the disc above its long, jagged teeth.

"We need to stop those trolls," hissed Eruptor. "They've almost got it."

But as the trolls reached forward for the key, its eyes snapped open.

"Thieves, thieves!" it yelled, in a voice like nails being scraped down a blackboard. "Somebody is coming to steal me. Get them!"

"Now, that's what I call a burglar alarm," commented Gill before his voice trailed off. Awoken by the Key's warning, the stone wyvern had sprung into life. Its hideous snout whipped up and twin beams of pure energy blazed out of its jewel-encrusted eyes, vapourising the first troll where he stood. His companion turned an even sicklier shade of green than usual, and turned to sprint back into the forest.

"He's getting away," screamed the Key. "Blast him!"

And the wyvern did exactly that. All was quiet

in the clearing again as the wyvern returned to its previous pose and the Key shut its eyes.

"So that's why Kaos was trying to turn trolls invisible," Spyro realised. "They'd be able to sneak up on the Key without it seeing them."

"True," agreed Gill, "but why didn't he use the spell on those two?"

Spyro frowned. Gill had a point.

"Never mind that," cut in Eruptor. "How are we supposed to nab it before that statue thing zaps us?"

All was quiet for a minute before a smile spread slowly across Spyro's face: "Listen up, fellas. I have a plan."

All was quiet in the clearing until Boomer burst out of the trees.

"Afternoon," the young troll called cheerfully. "Don't mind me. I'm just a thief come to steal the

Chattering Key."

The Key's eyes instantly flicked open.

"It's a thief," it cried out. "A dirty rotten robber. Fry him!"

The wyvern's eyes flared into life, but the energy beams struck harmlessly into the clearing floor. Boomer had leapt back undercover.

"Over there," the Key caterwauled as Eruptor jumped out of the trees to the right of the statue. "Another plunderer at three o'clock."

The wyvern's head spun around to face the lava monster but before it could unleash its deadly beams, the Key squawked again: "No, no. To the left. To the left!"

The wyvern twisted towards Gill who, at exactly the same moment, sprinted out of the foliage towards the Key.

"Don't shoot them," hollered Boomer as he poked his head back out of the branches straight in front of the statue "Yes, shoot him. I mean, shoot the one on the right. Or the left. Oh, shoot them all."

Spyro's plan was working perfectly. As the Key barraged the wyvern with conflicting commands, the living statue's head swung back and forth, not knowing which Skylander to destroy first. It was so confused that it didn't see Spyro shoot out of the trees behind the pyramid and snatch the Key from the wyvern's neck.

"Help!" the Chattering Key screeched. "I've been burglarised by a purple-scaled pilferer!"

The wyvern zeroed in on Spyro, who was flying as fast as his wings would carry him towards the trees.

"Any time now would be good, guys," Spyro called as he felt the wyvern's eye-beams zip over his head. Almost as one, the Skylanders turned on the statue. Eruptor unleashed a barrage of magma balls at the creature, while Gill blasted it with water. Just to make sure that the monster was completely disorientated, Boomer lobbed the triple-bound dynamite bundles he'd been saving for a special occasion at the wyvern's head. The troll let out a celebratory whoop when he saw one of his charges shatter the

gems embedded in the statue's eyes.

"Some use you were," the Key complained as Spyro crashed back into the trees. Spyro turned around quickly to make sure his friends were getting away and was satisfied to see them making their escape while the wyvern roared in frustration.

"Good work," Spyro praised as the Skylanders gathered around, back in the safety of the trees. "Now we just need to get this back to Flynn."

"You freakish filcherers don't think you've won that easily do you?" the Key scoffed, an evil grin flickering over its metallic face. "Oi! Fido, I'm over here. Fetch boy!"

"Fido!?" repeated a disbelieving Eruptor, as the Skylanders took to their heels. "What kind of name for a wyvern is Fido?"

"His kind of name by the looks of it," pointed out Gill as behind them the wyvern scrambled down from its perch and crashed blindly after them. "Run!"

CHAPTER NINE

THE TRAP

I t's amazing what having five-tonne of furious stone wyvern snapping at your heels will do for you. The Skylanders had never run so fast. They tore through the forest, tripping on brambles in their flight, while the statue ploughed through ancient tree trunks as if they were twigs.

Even the Fungus Rings of Despair didn't slow them. They were moving too fast to be affected by the spores.

"Perhaps that thing will be trapped in a nightmare of being pooped on by pigeons," offered Boomer, only to be shot down by the

Chattering Key.

"Don't bet on it, tea-leaf. Statues aren't known for their lungs. How is it going to breathe in the spores?"

Sure enough, the wyvern simply bulldozed its way through the toadstools without a flicker of fear. Boomer shoved a stick of dynamite into the Key's mouth for being such a smart aleck.

"One more word from you," the troll warned, "and I'll light it."

"You won't have the chance," grumbled Eruptor. "It's gaining on us."

Gill skid to a halt.

"What are you doing?" cried Spyro, but the Gillman just waved them on.

"I've got an idea," he announced, turning to face the wyvern and raising his water cannon.

"That won't stop it Gill."

"No, but it might slow it down a bit," Gill

cried out. "Let's just see if mud sticks around here."

Gill fired, not at the wyvern's body, but its feet. Almost instantly the forest floor became a quagmire. With a bellow, the creature slid, almost falling flat on its face. Within seconds, it was caked in the stuff.

"Eruptor, care to turn up the heat?" Gill asked, and the lava monster grinned. Without another word, he belched up a deluge of magma that sizzled as it flooded over the freezing cold mud. The wyvern wailed as the sludge on its legs hardened, holding it fast.

"Baked to perfection," said Eruptor as the wyvern struggled against the now rock-hard mud.

Boomer's eyes narrowed. The clay around the monster was already cracking.

"That won't hold it for long," he warned,

ignoring the muffled agreement of the Key, but Spyro wasn't worried.

"We're nearly there," the dragon insisted. "I can see the balloon."

"Flynn better have left the engine running," rumbled Eruptor.

But Flynn hadn't left the engine running. Flynn was currently tied-up from head to toe in thick, scratchy rope and hanging upside down from the grip of a titanic troll.

"Hello chaps," the pilot called sheepishly as the Skylanders piled out of the Forest. "I can explain everything."

"Let me," came a snivelling voice from behind the stricken Mabu. "It's all quite simple really. You lot have fallen into my quite brilliant trap."

"Kaos!" Spyro growled, his crest flattening against his head. "What trap?"

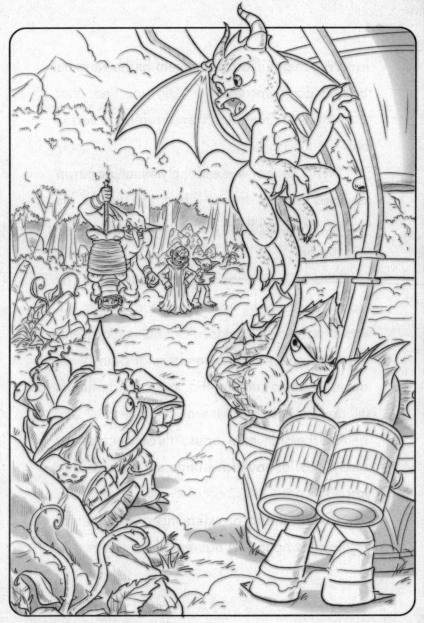

"What trap?" Kaos burst into laughter, tears running down his cheeks. "Did you hear that Glumshanks? They didn't even realise it was a trap."

"Well, to be honest," Flynn chipped in as Kaos's lanky butler loped up beside his master, "it would be a pretty useless trap if they did, baldy!"

"SIIILENCE!" Kaos raged, furious that, as usual, Glumshanks had got one over him. "It was a spectacular plan. A monumental plan. The most spectacular, monumental plan of all time. A plan so cunning that these dunderheads still don't realise what it was."

"Your plan," said Spyro through clenched teeth, "was to make it blindingly obvious that you were after the Chattering Key, so that Eon sent us after it and you didn't get it first."

"Then, when we'd braved all the dangers to

retrieve the thing . . ." continued Eruptor.

". . . you'd force us to hand it over in exchange for our friend, Flynn," added Gill before Boomer concluded with: "All you had to do is lie in wait."

"Sounds like the dunderheads have got it pretty sewn up," muttered Glumshanks, scratching the back of his neck.

"It doesn't matter," spat Kaos. "If they don't want to see their pilot pal turned into a tasty troll snack, they need to give me the Chattering Key right this minute."

"Don't do it, Spyro," called out Flynn, courageously. "It's true, the world will be a much bleaker place without me, and thousands of fair maidens will be weeping into their pillows tonight, but if you give Kaos that key, you'll be handing him ultimate power. And I really can't stand the creep!"

A shadow passed over Spyro's face.

"No," he said finally. "I'm not going to sacrifice you, Flynn. I'll give Kaos the key."

"What?" shrieked Kaos, "You dare to defy ME, Kaos, Lord of Darkness? You shall pay for this!"

The Skylanders frowned in unison as Glumshanks whispered into his master's ear.

"Er, sir? He said that he'd give you the key."

"He did?"

"Yeah, just then," Flynn chipped in. "We all heard him."

"Of course he did!" crowed Kaos excitedly, "I was just checking to see if you were all paying attention. Glumshanks, you go and get it from him."

Glumshanks clumped forward and took the key from Spyro, apologising under his breath. "I'm sorry. I keep telling him he needs to clear his ears out. He has a serious earwax condition."

"What did you say?" bellowed Kaos from behind.

"I just commented on the seriously good condition of this key," Glumshanks lied as he handed it over. "They don't make them like that anymore."

"AT LASSSST," Kaos exulted, holding the key above his head. "The Chattering Key is in my grasp. The secrets of the Ancient Ones will be MINE, ALL MINE!!"

The Key mumbled something against the stick of dynamite that was still wedged in its mouth.

"Looks like it's trying to tell you a secret now, master," Glumshanks pointed out as he reached over and yanked the explosive out of the Key's jaws.

"Thank you," said the Key gratefully, flexing its aching jaws. "That thing was killing me."

"What wisdom do you wish to impart,

ancient and mysterious artefact?" Kaos inquired, leaning in close. The Key wrinkled its nose.

"Just that you need a bath, little man. You are ripe!" the Key complained before yelling, "Fido! Follow your nose!"

From within the forest, the wyvern roared in reply and the Skylanders looked at each other as they heard an ominous cracking noise.

"It's breaking loose," Gill warned.

"No matter," said Kaos, shoving the key into Glumshanks' hands. "All I need to do is recite the ancient and mysterious incantation and the ancient and mysterious tomb will mysteriously and, er, well, anciently open." Kaos was frantically searching every pocket of his ratty, faded robes. "Glumshanks, where is the ancient and mysterious incantation?"

With a roll of his eyes, Glumshanks fished a

scrunched-up scrap of paper out from his own pocket and handed it to his master.

"Yes, of course, I gave it to you for safekeeping," fibbed Kaos, before straightening the paper and clearing his throat. From behind them, the sound of the approaching wyvern grew louder.

"It's free!" cried out Gill.

"Are you sitting comfortably?" Kaos asked with a smirk. "Then I shall begin:

'Oh ancient Arkeyans, I have the key,

And so you will give to me,

Everything my heart deserves,

Nowdoitquick,beforeyougetonmynerves.'"

As soon as Kaos had finished reciting the incantation, the ground beneath their feet began to shake. Spyro had to leap out of the way as a stone pillar burst out of the rock and rose into the air, a large keyhole carved into its side.

"BEHOLD," Kaos snatched the key back from his servant. "The ancient and mysterious lock."

Spyro wasn't sure what noise he hated more – the sound of the blind wyvern racing towards them or the triumph in Kaos's voice.

"I wouldn't put me in there if I were you," said the Key.

"Shut up," said Kaos as he stalked towards the pillar.

"You'll get everything you deserve," said the Key as it was raised to the keyhole.

"That's what I'm counting on," said Kaos as he thrust it into the lock.

"Me too," smirked the Key to itself.

With a roar, the Wyvern burst free of the forest. Everyone turned and froze in fear except for Kaos who was struggling in vain to turn the key in the lock, a vain pulsing on his egg-shaped head as he strained with the effort. Not taking his eyes from the wyvern, Glumshanks shoved his master aside and turned the key with ease.

The lock clicked once as the wyvern pounced.

CHAPTER TEN

THE PYRAMID OF JUST REWARDS

It had all happened so fast. One minute the Skylanders were waiting for the wyvern to come crashing down on them and the next a beam of light had shot from the pillar, blasting the living statue into a million fragments.

In front of them the forest was being churned up as a gargantuan pyramid rose out of the ground. Mighty oaks splintered as if they were firewood and hideous bat-like creatures shot up into the sky from their hiding places in the forest canopy.

Spyro rolled to the side to avoid being dragged onto the flight of stone steps that erupted from the base of the pillar up into the side of the pyramid.

Finally, when the pyramid had reached its zenith, all became still once again, save for the rocks, loose branches and dry soil that slid down the structure's smooth sides.

"Even I have to admit that was kinda impressive," whistled Eruptor.

High above their heads, the clouds spiralled around the pyramid's peak, which Spyro recognised as the wyvern's perch from the clearing. Had this really all been buried beneath the forest all this time? Lightning reflected against its polished surface.

"Who dares raise the Pyramid of Just Rewards?" boomed a deafening voice that seemed to come from high above.

"That'll be me," squeaked Kaos, beside himself with glee. "I dare."

"Do you deserve what you will be given?"

"Absolutely," replied Kaos eagerly. "Without question!"

"Then enter of your own free will." Two colossal doors swung open at the top of the stairs. "And woe betide anyone who follows you within."

"Ha!" shouted Kaos, pointing straight at Spyro. "Did you hear that? Woe betide. That means YOU, dragonfly."

"We'll stop you if it's the last thing we do, Kaos," promised Spyro, only to be rewarded by another wave of manic laughter from the victorious Portal Master.

"You and whose army, Skychumps? I'm about to lay my hands on an ancient and mysterious weapon of ancient and mysterious power.

I will be UNSTOPPABLE and you will be DOOOOOOMED!!."

"Er, sir," said Glumshanks, sidling up to Kaos. "Perhaps we should get up there and get the ancient and mysterious weapon before they realise that they could just knock us from this staircase before we get to the door?"

"Idiot!" screamed Kaos. "Whose side are you on anyway? I'd already thought of that. Trolls, bring that puffed up excuse of a pilot. If the Skyflunkees try anything, throw him from the stairs and watch his poor broken body smash against the sides of the pyramid. Bwa-ha-ha-HAAAAA!"

Eruptor bristled. "I can take him Spyro. All it would take is one magma ball."

"Cool it, Eruptor," Gill warned, "Kaos isn't joking. He's crazy enough to chuck Flynn over the edge."

"Yeah," added Boomer, "and even though Flynn is full of more hot air than one of his balloons, I doubt the guy will float."

"Don't worry Flynn," Spyro shouted as the pilot was dragged up the stairs. "We'll save you."

Flynn didn't answer. He was too busy shouting "Ow!" every time his head hit a stone step, which was happening a lot. Kaos meanwhile had made it to the top. Wheezing with the effort, he turned for some last-minute gloating.

"See you when I'm the lord of all, Skyflops," he panted, before nearly losing his balance and pitching forward. Lucky for him (although not for the fate of the universe) Glumshanks was on hand to leap forward, catch him and haul him back up. Without even stopping to say thank you, Kaos disappeared across the threshold, followed by his trolls dragging the now nearly unconscious Flynn.

The heavy stone doors swung shut with a bang.

Spyro was the first to react. "Come on," he ordered as he charged to the bottom of the staircase.

"Woah there, dragon-boy," the Key said as Spyro sped past. "I don't think you want to go in there."

Spyro slid to a halt.

"What do you mean?" he asked.

"What I said. You. Don't. Want. To. Go. In. There."

"But I need to," Spyro insisted, as the rest of his friends caught up with him.

"You mean, WE need to," corrected Gill. "How many times do you have to be reminded that you don't have to do everything by yourself?"

"Oh, I know the type," the Key commented. "Always jumping in before looking? A real hot head?"

"The worst," confirmed Eruptor, ignoring the look that Spyro gave him.

"You can talk!"

"Hey, if the cap fits . . ."

"Guys, guys!" Gill positioned himself between his two friends, trying to calm the situation before they both blew their tops. "This isn't helping, OK?"

"Nothing will," said the Key. "You might as well head home. You're done here."

"Can I blow that thing up now?" asked Boomer, his eyes narrowing on the Key.

"Maybe," Spyro stalked towards the Key, smoke puffing from his nostrils, "unless it opens the doors for us."

In a flash, Boomer had a stick of dynamite in his hand and a wicked look on his face.

"Wait!" shrieked the Key. "I couldn't open up those doors if I wanted to! Not now that the chosen one is inside."

"The chosen one?" spluttered Gill. "You mean Kaos?"

"If that's what he calls himself. He's chosen this path and will get what he deserves. You can't stop that from happening."

"But he's got our friend!" cut in Boomer, wagging the stick of dynamite in the Key's face.

"We can't just leave."

A look of concern flashed over the Key's face for a second. When it spoke again, its voice was full of sympathy. "Look, I can see why this is difficult for you, but trust me. There's nothing you can do. You really don't want to go in there!"

"Yes we do," Spyro hissed, turning back towards the stairs, "and we'll do it with or without your help. Boomer, you wanted to blow something up?"

"Yeah?"

"Blow up the doors."

Boomer whooped, kicked his heels together in joy and started to skip up the steps, his hands suddenly full of explosives. Spyro never liked to think where he kept his supplies.

"Wait, wait, wait," screamed the Key. "There's no need to do that!"

"You'll help us then?"

"Yes," the Key agreed with a sigh. "But only for two reasons. Number one, those doors are completely bomb proof so you'll be there all day, and the racket will bring on one of my migraines."

Boomer's grin vanished.

"And two, I don't like the thought of anyone being down there when Kaos receives his prize. You have to promise me that you'll just grab your friend and get out. No heroics."

"You have our word," said Gill, although Spyro could see that the Gillman had crossed his webbed-fingers behind his back.

"OK, just don't tell anyone I've done this. I have a reputation to protect." The Key strained in the lock, although the doors at the top of the stairs remained firmly shut. "There," he finally said, "All done."

"But the doors . . ." Spyro started, only to be

interrupted by the Key.

". . . Are still closed, yes I know. I meant what I said – no one will ever pass that way again. I've opened the tradesmen's entrance, round the back."

"Round the back?" whined Eruptor, taking in the full scale of the pyramid. "Have you seen the size of this thing?"

"Then we better get going," shouted Spyro as he took off. Still moaning, Eruptor lumbered after him, with Boomer close behind, bombs in hand.

"Thanks dude," said Gill, giving the Key a friendly pat on the head before setting off after his friends. "We owe you one."

"Don't thank me yet," the Key said sadly as soon as they were out of earshot. "I may have just opened the door to your destruction."

CHAPTER ELEVEN

BEHOLD, THE MACHINE OF DOOM

The Key had been as good as its word. When they'd finally reached the other side of the pyramid they'd found a tiny door only just big enough to squeeze through. Despite his grumbles, Eruptor insisted on leading the way, his warm glow lighting up the claustrophobic corridor.

"Don't think much of whoever decorated this place," Gill commented as they crept forward.

"Macabre and moody is so last season."

Spyro glanced at the pictures carved into the stone walls. Mighty machines of war crushed piles of screaming skulls while Arkeyan warriors stood victorious over their enemies. His mood darkened. If Kaos had already claimed his prize...

After what seemed like an eternity of scrambling up the narrow corridor, the Skylanders emerged onto some kind of balcony.

"Wow!" whispered Boomer, peeking over

the edge. "That's some serious hardware."

The robot must have been four metres tall and stood in the middle of a wide, flame-filled moat. Every rivet in its thick armour plating was illuminated in a beam of dazzling light, vicious-looking spikes erupting across its broad shoulders. Worst of all was its massive horned head. The face was a blank mask save for two slits for eyes.

It looked completely and utterly evil.

"It's the most beautiful thing I've ever seen," Boomer gushed, his eyes glistening at the sight of the gigantic cannons and rocket launchers mounted on its powerful pneumatic arms. "Just think of the damage you could do."

The troll's eyes rested on a glass panel set into the machine's chest. Behind it sat an array of complicated controls and levers. Boomer's fingers twitched at the thought of finding out

how it all worked. All he would need to do was climb the ladder of floating stepping-stones that rose from the marble floor below.

"Think of the damage Kaos could do, you mean?" Gill reminded the eager troll.

As if on cue, the elaborate wooden doors that led into the chamber below smashed open and Kaos tumbled in, still wheezing heavily.

"When I'm supreme overlord," he croaked, gasping for air, "I'm installing an elevator in this thing." Then the minuscule Portal Master laid his eyes on the towering giant and clapped his hands together in pleasure.

"Glumshanks, look at it. I mean, really look at it. It's as deadly-looking as the ancient scrolls described."

"Not bad," sniffed Glumshanks, as he plodded into the chamber, followed by the rest of the trolls who were still dragging the increasingly battered Flynn.

"Not bad?" repeated Kaos, his voice squeaking with indignation. "Glumshanks, this is the Machine of Doom, the most dangerous weapon ever created. Nothing can stand in this baby's way. Not Eon, not the Core of Light and definitely not that pitiful flying worm, Spyro."

Spyro's face reddened and his spines flattened against his skin. Suddenly he felt a cool, damp hand against his shoulder.

"I know that look," Gill whispered in his ear, "but flying in head first won't solve anything."

"Especially if he has that STINKING SPRAT of a pet fish with him," added Kaos in an even louder voice.

"Stinking?" Gill bristled immediately and, forgetting his own advice, vaulted over the balcony. "Who are you calling stinking?"

With a wet slap, Gill landed on his feet

and brought up his water cannon to fix Kaos in his sights. "I'll have you know that personal hygiene is very important to me."

"Well, that's our cover blown," shrugged Eruptor and pitched over the edge to land beside his amphibious compadre. "What do you say, Gill? Fancy turning up the heat?"

"An excellent idea," squealed Kaos with delight, strangely unperturbed by the sudden appearance of the Skylanders. It was almost as if he was expecting them. "Glumshanks, are you ready to SLIP another WIMP on the barbie? GLUMSHAAANKS!?!"

"Over here master. Doing your bidding. As always."

From his vantage point, Spyro saw Glumshanks suspend the bound Flynn over the flames that surrounded the Machine of Doom.

Flynn, for his own part, started trying

desperately to blow out the raging furnace with ineffectual little puffs.

"Well, blow me down," Kaos simpered, adopting a stance of mock desperation. "Stalemate. I wonder what will happen next?"

"How about I blow something up?"

"Boomer, no!" The troll moved too quickly for Spyro. He flung himself off the balcony and tumbled through the air, sending bombs spiralling out in all directions. The resulting explosions echoed around the chamber, forcing Spyro to cover his ears. When the cacophony had died down, he looked up to see Boomer racing towards the stepping-stones that led up to the robot's expansive chest. He was going to try to take control of the Machine of Doom.

"NOOO!" Kaos wailed, hurtling after the scampering troll. "Somebody stop him before it's too late." But Kaos' minions already had their hands full dealing with Gill and Eruptor. Water spouts and lava flows were shooting everywhere as Boomer reached the bottom step.

At any other time, Spyro would have joined the fray by now, but something was nagging away at him. This didn't seem right. Kaos was acting weirdly, even for him. Spyro launched himself into the air and glided down to his fellow Skylanders.

"Guys, listen up," he shouted, struggling to make himself heard over the sounds of battle. "I don't like this. Something smells fishy."

"Don't you start!" warned Gill as he blasted a nearby troll. "Anyway, this is too easy – like shooting fish in a barrel."

"Exactly. It isn't right."

"What are you talking about?" Eruptor bellowed between brimstone-filled belches. "Are you going to kick troll butt or what?"

"No, and neither are you," Spyro commanded. "Hold your fire!"

"Are you crazy?"

"I mean it Eruptor. Just stop for a minute."

Eruptor did what he was told and Gill let his finger off the trigger. Spyro turned to face the trolls.

"See," he said, his eyes narrowed. "They're not attacking. They weren't even fighting back."

The Skylanders looked at the trolls and the trolls looked at the Skylanders and then everyone looked at the Machine of Doom.

Boomer was nearly at the top of the stairs.

"Don't you DARE," yelped Kaos as he tripped over his own feet and landed flat on his face.

"Whoops!" But as the Portal Master struggled back up, Spyro could see that he was grinning from ear to ear.

"He wants Boomer to get to the Machine of Doom," Spyro realised with a start. "Boomer, wait!"

As the tech-loving troll reached the top of the stairs, a voice loud enough to rattle the teeth in their jaws reverberated around the chamber.

"Behold, the Machine of Doom," it bellowed. "The most devastating weapon ever created."

"Told you," Kaos pointed out to a cringing Glumshanks.

"Who claims this weapon?"

"Well, I was going to," piped up Kaos, "but that disgusting little troll has pipped me to the post."

"Is that true, troll," boomed the voice, "Do you claim the Machine of Doom?"

"Yeah oh yeah oh yeah," babbled Boomer

excitedly. "That wimp down there won't stand a chance against this thing."

"Are you sure?" the voice asked.

"No," shouted Spyro. "He's not."

But Boomer wasn't listening.

"120 per cent sure," Boomer announced. "Times two. Actually, scratch that. Times infinity."

"Then fulfill your destiny. Your fate is in your own hands."

The glass panel in the Machine of Doom's chest slid up and Boomer somersaulted over the controls and settled into the expansive chair. Pistons hissed and steam bellowed out of every joint as the metal titan came to life, its eyes blazing with red fire. As Boomer fiddled furiously with the controls, one of its massive hands swung up and swatted the stepping-stones away.

"Way to go Boomer," cheered Eruptor, waving at his friend, but Spyro wasn't celebrating.

"Don't you get it, Eruptor? This isn't right."

"Of course it is!" Gill insisted. "We've stopped Kaos. We've saved the day."

"No, we haven't." Spyro said sadly. "We've done exactly what he wanted."

"Oh, look Glumshanks," Kaos cackled from the foot of the robot. "The penny has finally dropped. Dragonfly has worked out that they've fallen into my trap. Again!"

CHAPTER TWELVE

A TRAP WITHIN A TRAP

Boomer was in trouble. From behind the control panel, the troll was frantically pulling levers and pressing buttons, but nothing seemed to be working. All around him, the Machine of Doom creaked and groaned.

This wasn't quite what he'd expected. The robot had looked perfect. Destructive, malignant and hazardous to everyone's health, yes, but perfect all the same. It should have been the ideal deterrent in the fight against Kaos. There was no way he would dare to attack the Core of Light if it was protected by the Machine of Doom, but as Boomer struggled to control the shuddering colossus the only word he could use to describe the robot was . . . junk.

A section of pipe above Boomer's head burst, a spray of scolding steam narrowly missing his ears. He yelped and yanked a large, red lever to his right, only for it to come off in his hand. The control panel erupted into a shower of sparks.

Far below, at the foot of the juddering automaton, Kaos was beside himself, tears pouring down his face as he clutched his aching sides. He laughed so much that he nearly choked.

Eruptor wasn't laughing. Instead he was staring in disbelief at the Machine of Doom, which looked like it was coming apart at the

seams. Its head had lolled to the side and dark smoke billowed from its neck. As the Skylanders watched in disbelief, its heavy right arm detached from an armour-clad shoulder and crashed to the chamber floor, sending up a huge plume of dust.

"What's Boomer doing?" Eruptor spluttered. "I thought there wasn't a machine he couldn't master?"

"He never stood a chance with that thing," Spyro replied, fixing Kaos with a glare. "Isn't that right Kaos?"

The Portal Master stopped chuckling and smirked knowingly at the dragon.

"Well, let's just consider the evidence shall we? We're in the Pyramid of Just Rewards, the last resting place of a device believed to be capable of destroying anything in its path. Then there were all those cracks about me getting what I deserved and the big, booming voice banging on about fate and destiny . . ."

"The Machine of Doom was never real was it?" Spyro asked, cutting Kaos off. "It was a trap designed to capture anyone who might be tempted to steal a weapon capable of destroying the Core of Light."

"The Arkeyans were a clever bunch," Kaos confirmed. "Almost as clever as me. They knew that anyone crazy enough to brave their worst nightmares in the Forest of Fear, sneaky enough to steal the Chattering Key from the stone wyvern and batty enough to climb into an all-powerful super-weapon was too dangerous to walk free."

"The dumpy one speaks the truth," boomed the voice of the pyramid. "You have made your choice and must live with the consequences."

"Ignoring the dumpy comment for one minute," Kaos yelled back at the ceiling, "by

consequences do you mean that this entire pyramid is about to fall on our heads, burying us alive?"

"That is correct."

"Thought so. Thanks for clearing that up. Much obliged."

"You knew all the time, didn't you?" Spyro asked as the ground beneath their feet began to quake. "You knew the truth about the Machine of Doom."

"Oh Spyro, do you really expect me to explain my entire fiendish plan like some second-rate, tin-pot villain?"

"Yes."

"Fair enough. Of course I realised what would happen if someone tried to steal the Machine of Doom. You have to get up pretty early in the morning to get one over on Kaos. I knew if you thought I was trying to steal it, you would try to stop me . . . "

". . . And you could trick us into seizing the Machine of Doom ourselves . . ." rumbled Eruptor.

". . . Thereby springing the trap of the Ancient Arkeyans," completed Gill, as rubble started to tumble down from the ceiling.

"Finally, they get it," crowed Kaos, slipping his hand inside his cloak. "Top of the class boys."

"There's one problem with your plan,"

 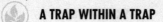
pointed out Spyro, jumping into the air to escape the yawning crack that had sprung open beneath his feet.

"The fact that I'll be trapped here with you?" Kaos asked innocently. "Yes, it did cross my simply staggering mind, which is why I invented . . . THIS."

Kaos threw a small box into the air. It hovered for a second before bursting into bright green light.

"Gentlemen, may I introduce my latest invention?" Kaos announced, as the cube began to unfold. "The compact, convenient, completely and utterly portable travel portal. Accept no substitutes. Patent pending."

With a thud the now fully-grown Portal slammed down to the trembling floor and flared into life.

"Instant travel back to any secret lair you

choose. Come on boys, it's time to skedaddle."

All around, the trolls started racing towards the portal, leaping over the fissures in the marble floor below and avoiding the crushing feet of the chaotic robot above. One by one they leapt onto its surface and vanished.

"We'll be leaving you now," gloated Kaos, "I'd like to say it was fun."

"You need to take us with you," yelled Spyro as a huge section of masonry narrowly missed him before crashing to the floor.

"Hmmm, let me think about that." Kaos

actually seemed to consider it before a spiteful smile stretched across his face. "Nah, don't think so. Glumshanks, we're off!"

"But what about this guy?" the butler shouted, still suspending Flynn above the leaping flames.

"Let him roast. You can eat later."

Glumshanks shrugged, released the rope and pelted for the portal. With a terrified yell, Flynn plummeted towards the fire.

Eruptor was off like a shot, rolling himself towards the moat like a demented bowling ball. He toppled over the edge, straight into the fire and caught Flynn before the flames

could do any real damage. In a flash, Gill was beside them, dousing the pilot's smouldering clothes with water from his pack.

It was just the distraction Glumshanks needed. The gangly troll was through the portal before anyone could stop him. Spyro knew he had to move quickly. As soon as Kaos escaped, the portal would be useless. He prepared to pounce, but Kaos spun around, magical energy crackling from his fingertips.

"Oh no you don't, Spyro."

The lightning lanced across the already weakened floor, splitting it in two. Giant flames plumed into the air between Spyro and the portal. "Nice try, Skyfool," Kaos shrieked, "but you are, to coin a phrase, doomed. Enjoy being BURIED ALIVE!!"

CHAPTER THIRTEEN

ESCAPE

The Machine of Doom's bulky fist smashed down from above, crushing the portal beneath its steel-capped knuckles. Kaos let out a noise that was somewhere between a scream and a squeak, and looked up. The giant, one-armed robot loomed over them. It had lost its head and looked on the brink of breaking apart but in the middle of the control cabin, Boomer was sitting in a spider's web of cables, which he yanked this way and that.

"Sorry about that," the troll apologized over

the robot's loudspeaker system, a wild grin plastered across his face. "It took a while to rewire this thing, but I've got the hang of it now."

"No!" shouted Kaos, falling to his knees beside the pulverized escape route. "My compact, convenient, completely and utterly portable travel portal. What have you done?"

"Fellas, I don't think this lash up will last forever," Boomer yelled over the noise of the collapsing pyramid. "If we're going to get out of here, we have to do it now."

"What are we waiting for then?" bellowed Eruptor. "Give us a hand up."

Boomer yanked the cables to his right and the Machine of Doom's remaining arm swung around. Eruptor and Gill helped Flynn onto the robot's upturned palm and were carried high into the air to join Boomer in the control cabin.

"Are you coming Spyro?" Gill shouted down

as Boomer pointed the automaton's massive cannon at the floor.

Spyro looked at his friends and then to Kaos who was scrabbling around on his knees, desperately trying to piece together his portal. He knew Kaos deserved to be left here in the very same trap he'd tried to spring, but he also knew what Master Eon would do. Making his decision, the little purple dragon launched himself into the air and, as he swooped by, grabbed Kaos by his cloak. His wings straining

with the load, Spyro flew towards his friends,
dodging falling masonry and tumbling beams.
Just when he thought he couldn't make it, he saw
Gill reaching down to him. He spun in mid-air,
thrust his tail high and felt the Gillman's hands
grab hold. Gill hauled Spyro and Kaos into
the control cabin as Boomer fired the cannon
straight into the chamber floor.

The recoil from the cannon blasted the Machine of Doom up into the air. It rocketed through the collapsing ceiling and burst out into the night sky. Beneath them, the pyramid finally tumbled into a pit.

For a second, it felt like they were hovering high above the devastation.

And then gravity took hold.

The Machine of Doom finally broke apart as they plummeted down. The Skylanders clutched onto anything they could as they fell, screaming all the way (except for Boomer, who seemed to love every minute).

For the second time that day the ground rushed up to greet them and . . .

WOOMPH!

Spyro opened his eyes to see Gill sprawled on his back, laughing hysterically. To his right Eruptor was standing on his head, while Boomer was leaping up and down on the thick, springy cloud that had broken their fall.

"Again, again!" the troll yelled as Flynn took off his flying helmet and scratched his head.

"Almost as good as one of my landings."

A shadow fell over Spyro. He turned to see Eon silhouetted against the moon. The Portal Master waved his staff and the mist he'd conjured to catch them faded away.

"Are you well, young dragon?" Eon asked as they were gently lowered to the ground.

Spyro broke into a massive grin. "I am now. But how did you get here?"

"I'm not sure exactly what you've been up to, but the fog that shrouds the Forest of Fear cleared enough for me to open a portal."

"Wait a minute," chimed in Eruptor. "Where's 'short, pale and ugly'?"

"Kaos!" Spyro remembered, looking around the crash site. Their adversary was nowhere to be seen.

"He got away?" moaned Boomer. "After all that?"

"You told us not to underestimate him," Spyro remembered. "I won't do it again."

"We all underestimated Kaos," Eon said solemnly. "Myself included. By the looks of things he's more dangerous than ever and he won't rest until he's destroyed the Core of Light."

"That's a shame," rumbled Eruptor, "because, boy, does he ever need his beauty sleep."

Spyro couldn't help but smile, although he knew Eon was right. This was only the beginning. Kaos would strike again, but next time they'd be ready.

"What a ride, though," whistled Gill. "It's not every day you face invisible trolls, get chased by living statues and escape inescapable traps."

"I don't know," said Spyro with a laugh. "Sounds like the norm to me."

Gill wasn't having any of it. "I still think it's the kind of day they'll write songs about."

Eruptor's face fell. "Don't you dare, fishface."

"In fact I think I'll start now . . ."

And with that, Gill Grunt began to sing.

EPILOGUE

Glumshanks poked his head around the door.

"Do you need anything else before bed, Master?" he inquired, only to have a mug of hot cocoa thrown in his general direction. The china smashed on the doorframe, splattering the butler in steaming brown liquid. "I'll take that as a no."

The troll shut the door behind him.

In the middle of his evil lair, sitting in his evil chair by his evil fireplace, Kaos sat and sulked an evil sulk.

It had been a foolproof plan and yet those

goody-goody-two-shoe-wearing Skylosers had managed to escape.

At least they hadn't captured him. At the last minute, as they'd tumbled from the sky, he'd managed to activate a fragment of the compact, convenient, completely and utterly portable travel portal and got himself home.

Still, he could imagine them laughing at him from Eon's ivory tower.

They'll be laughing on the other side of their faces soon enough.

Kaos grabbed a heavy book from his side-table, cursed as it slipped through his fingers and swore loudly as it landed on his stockinged foot. Rubbing his aching toes, Kaos heaved the book back onto his lap and read the words emblazoned on the dark, leather cover.

"101 Ways to Become Lord of Skylands."

With a bitter snarl, he flicked the book open, snatched up a pencil and scribbled out the words on the first page: 'Plan One: The Machine of Doom'.

Then the corners of Kaos' thin, cruel mouth twitched into a smile. The smile turned into a smirk and the smirk turned into a manic giggle. This wasn't the end. It was only the beginning. Kaos turned the page . . .

THE END?